Shirley Barber's
SPELLBOUND
A Fairytale Romance

The Five Mile Press

Shirley Barber's
SPELLBOUND
A Fairytale Romance

$\mathcal{O}$nce upon a time some fairy folk lived in a little town by a sparkling stream. Their tiny houses were built among mossy boulders, half hidden by drooping ferns. The fairy King and Queen lived with their two daughters in a palace made of leaves and petals and with vine-clad balconies overlooking the water.

Princess Rowena was dark-eyed and raven-haired, and little Lisette was the fairest of all the golden fairies. But Princess Lisette was so sweet-natured and so lovely to look upon that Princess Rowena, though equally beautiful, became troubled by envy and deeply unhappy.

The King was kept busy with the affairs of his kingdom, and the Queen by her younger children, so neither noticed their daughter's unhappiness.

$\mathcal{P}$rincess Rowena was some years older
than Princess Lisette, and had helped to care for her as a
child. But as the little golden fairy grew into a beautiful
young girl, so too did the envy grow in her elder sister.

Princess Rowena had found she was able to cast spells,
which was a rare and valued gift among her people. She
knew she should never misuse her gift to harm others,
but gradually her envy overcame her better feelings. She
ordered a golden armlet to be made, and as the jewels
were set in it she imbued it with a powerful spell.

One evening, Rowena gave her sister
the magic armlet. Lisette exclaimed with delight as its
jewels sparkled in the lamplight. "I shall always wear it,
dear Rowena," she promised, as she slid it upon her
arm. "It is so sweet of you, but then, you have always
been such a kind sister to me."

Rowena went to stand for a while on
the balcony and gazed down at the moonlit water. She
knew that while her beautiful sister was bound by the
spell in the armlet she would become tired and unable to
fly as a fairy should. The envy within her was satisfied,
but her heart was heavy for she knew she had
done a great wrong.

$\mathcal{N}$ow, in a neighbouring kingdom, two handsome princes were bidding farewell to their father and mother in an airy palace suspended between pink and white foxglove spires. They were about to set out on a journey to find two fairy brides.

"Choose wisely," commanded King Aven. "They must be of royal blood, and beautiful, if possible, for the sake of our people —"

"— and sweet-natured," put in Queen Bel, "so that I may find it easy to love them."

"Healthy and strong," continued the King, "for they must fly with you and help you to care for the fairy people in your kingdom. Remember, Burnet, this kingdom among the foxgloves shall be yours one day, and you, Trefoil, shall have the meadowsweet realm on the banks of the stream."

The princes flew off, together with several
servants carrying provisions for the journey. Prince Burnet had
heard that two beautiful princesses lived downstream, and a
honeybee told him where to find them.

"They live downstream among the ferns," he buzzed.
"I z-z-zee them when I fly down for a drink of water."

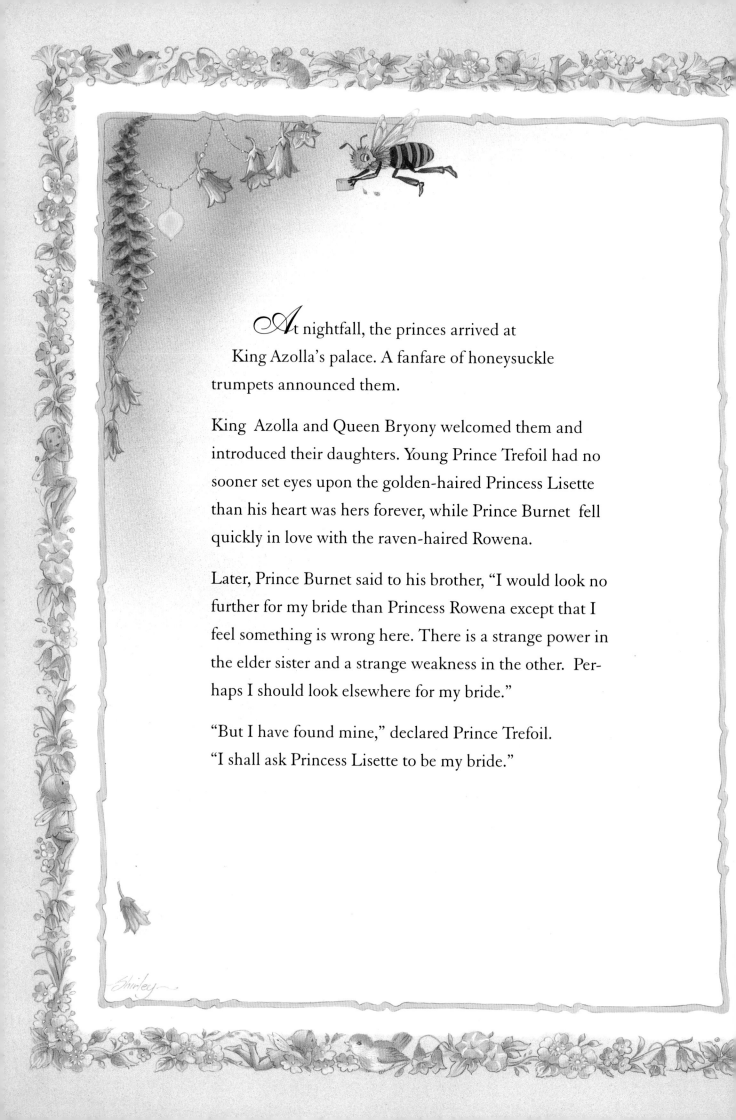

At nightfall, the princes arrived at King Azolla's palace. A fanfare of honeysuckle trumpets announced them.

King Azolla and Queen Bryony welcomed them and introduced their daughters. Young Prince Trefoil had no sooner set eyes upon the golden-haired Princess Lisette than his heart was hers forever, while Prince Burnet fell quickly in love with the raven-haired Rowena.

Later, Prince Burnet said to his brother, "I would look no further for my bride than Princess Rowena except that I feel something is wrong here. There is a strange power in the elder sister and a strange weakness in the other. Perhaps I should look elsewhere for my bride."

"But I have found mine," declared Prince Trefoil. "I shall ask Princess Lisette to be my bride."

The next day, Prince Trefoil found Lisette walking among the violets, and gently asked her to marry him. Lisette hung her golden head sadly. "Alas, dear Prince," she sighed. "I don't know why, but I have become too weak to fly. I cannot be your bride, as I would be unable to work alongside you in your kingdom."

Prince Trefoil stood awhile in serious thought, then came to a decision. "Sweet Princess, you are the only one for me. Tomorrow, I shall tell my parents that I must give up my kingdom. It is true that a prince must marry a princess who is able to fly, but an ordinary fairy may marry his true love, whether she can fly or not!"

Then he flew away to ask her father for her hand in marriage.

Once he was out of sight,
Princess Lisette shed bitter tears.
"I cannot let my dear Prince ruin his life for me,"
she sobbed. "I shall go far away where he can't find me.
Then perhaps he will forget me and marry
another fairy who can fly."

She walked out over the floating leaves of
water plants and stepped into a fallen leaf. She pushed
it into the middle of the stream where the fast-flowing
current carried her swiftly down the valley.

Meanwhile, King Azolla and the two princes spent much time in anxious talk. The King praised Trefoil for the strength of his love, but said he must not give up his kingdom without consulting his parents.

Suddenly, word came that Princess Lisette was missing. They all joined in the search for her, but she was nowhere to be found.

After several days of searching, all hope of finding her was gone, but the heart-broken Prince Trefoil announced he would keep looking until he found her. Nothing his brother or the King and Queen said could make him change his mind, and he flew away alone, down the valley into wild regions where no fairies had ventured before.

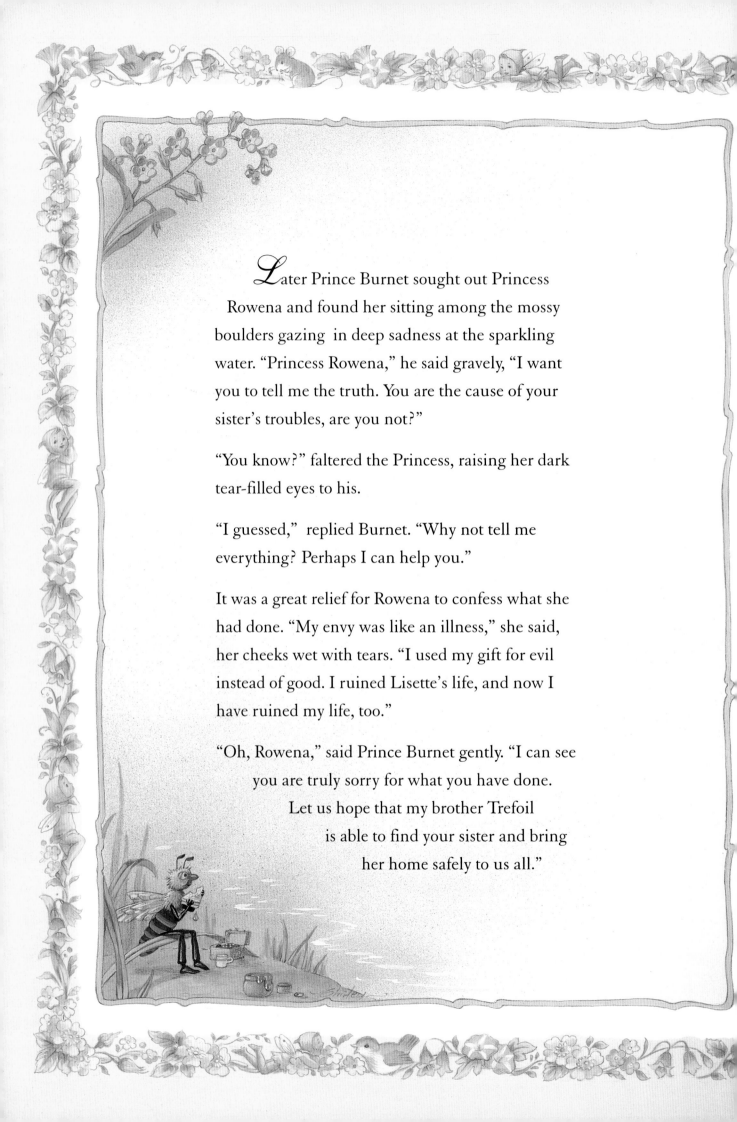

$\mathcal{L}$ater Prince Burnet sought out Princess Rowena and found her sitting among the mossy boulders gazing in deep sadness at the sparkling water. "Princess Rowena," he said gravely, "I want you to tell me the truth. You are the cause of your sister's troubles, are you not?"

"You know?" faltered the Princess, raising her dark tear-filled eyes to his.

"I guessed," replied Burnet. "Why not tell me everything? Perhaps I can help you."

It was a great relief for Rowena to confess what she had done. "My envy was like an illness," she said, her cheeks wet with tears. "I used my gift for evil instead of good. I ruined Lisette's life, and now I have ruined my life, too."

"Oh, Rowena," said Prince Burnet gently. "I can see you are truly sorry for what you have done. Let us hope that my brother Trefoil is able to find your sister and bring her home safely to us all."

$\mathcal{P}$rincess Lisette had been carried a long way
downstream and soon her leafboat began to sink.
She managed to struggle ashore and found herself
in a sheltered inlet. Here she rested in the shade of
tangled vines which were weighed down with ripe
berries upon which she fed.

Many tiny froglets who lived among the reeds came
shyly out to talk to her, and as the days passed they
became her little friends. They told her it was a good
place to stay and that there was only one
danger: sometimes a dragon would rise from the
water to snap at flies — and froglets, if he could
catch them!

"Perhaps he might even eat a fairy!" said one froglet. "If
he should come you must run away and hide as we do."

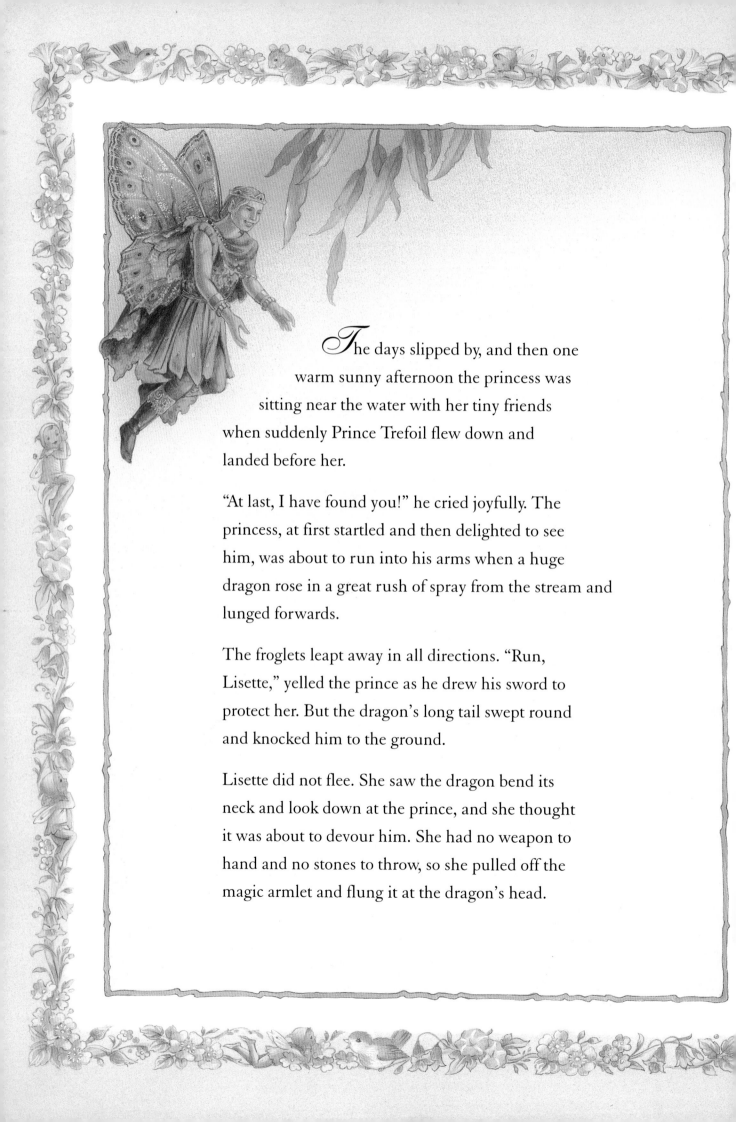

The days slipped by, and then one warm sunny afternoon the princess was sitting near the water with her tiny friends when suddenly Prince Trefoil flew down and landed before her.

"At last, I have found you!" he cried joyfully. The princess, at first startled and then delighted to see him, was about to run into his arms when a huge dragon rose in a great rush of spray from the stream and lunged forwards.

The froglets leapt away in all directions. "Run, Lisette," yelled the prince as he drew his sword to protect her. But the dragon's long tail swept round and knocked him to the ground.

Lisette did not flee. She saw the dragon bend its neck and look down at the prince, and she thought it was about to devour him. She had no weapon to hand and no stones to throw, so she pulled off the magic armlet and flung it at the dragon's head.

The spinning armlet flashed in the sunlight,
and the dragon snapped at it and swallowed it whole. Then,
its magic spell began to work, and sapped him of his strength.
He fell back into the stream and sank slowly into its depths,
never to return.

The dragon's claw had wounded Prince Trefoil, but Princess Lisette made bandages of cobwebs and healing salves from streamside herbs. As he regained his strength, so too did she recover hers and she soon found that she could fly once more. At last, the day came for them to say goodbye to their froglet friends, and together they flew up the valley to the fern kingdom of King Azolla.

What cheers and rejoicing took place when they arrived! A huge feast was prepared to welcome them, and there it was announced that Princess Rowena would marry Prince Burnet, while Princess Lisette would marry her beloved Trefoil. In a moment of quiet, Rowena spoke sorrowfully to her sister of her wrong-doing, and begged for her forgiveness. Lisette lovingly forgave her, and together the two couples planned happily for their wedding.

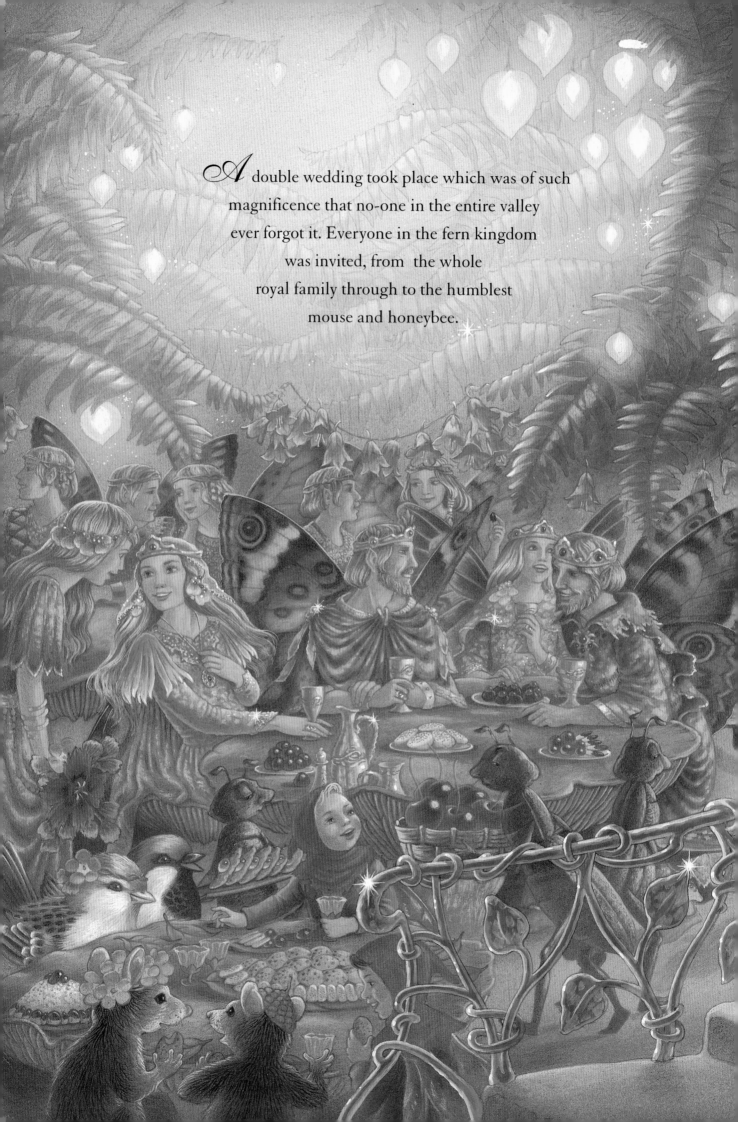

A double wedding took place which was of such
magnificence that no-one in the entire valley
ever forgot it. Everyone in the fern kingdom
was invited, from the whole
royal family through to the humblest
mouse and honeybee.

The happy fairy couples flew
away to their new homes among
the foxgloves and meadowsweet.

Princess Rowena only used her gift
for the good of others — so the fairy folk
lived happily ever after.

And the dragon who had swallowed the armlet
lay spellbound at the bottom of the stream, never to
frighten the froglets again.